A Dying Art

Sasha Faulks

For all my beloved souls

Contents

.

Pawel's Song of Life

'Old age doth reduce us from conquering kings
to pitiful porters who have lost the keys to a
great library of wisdom'

IT STARTED WITH A STROKE, OR SO THEY SAID.

I told them I had experienced a strange popping sensation in my head one night which may have woken me up, and from then on I began to notice the most significant change in my ability to think clearly, to remember things, to put the right word to the right object.

Then there was the paperboy.

That was the damnedest thing. I spotted him at the gate (I was peering round the edge of my curtain) whistling a tune. The tune didn't worry me as I'm sure it wasn't one I had heard before, probably some incantation of the young. There was a time when youngsters carried small cassette boxes with them— *Walkmen* (there, I've remembered that)—which were annoying enough because you could hear the sound leaking out of them like someone kicking a can up an alley. Now the boxes are more discreet and appear to function as phones and miniature TVs, and the sound, thankfully, remains a personal experience. It's clever, undoubtedly, but the sight of the white wires permanently trailing from people's heads unnerves me and occasionally catches me out. It's possible they could be undergoing some sort of brain experiment—an illicit one which might one day be exposed on *Panorama*—and only I could see it. On the other hand, they could just be plugged in to the latest gadget.

The tune the paperboy was whistling was, as I've said, immaterial. But the words 'paperboy' and 'newspaper' were the bugbears. They were gone from my mental repertoire: out of reach, like berries on a bush behind railings. You pushed your childhood fingers through and wiggled them for extension but you just couldn't get there.

'What do you call the chap with the thing, God damn it, the black-and-white thing?'

When I exposed this confusion to someone else, Mrs Grayling from next door, it was mortifying. She is a decent woman, but I think she fills buns with custard for a living, whereas I had been an engineer, and relatively highly regarded for that. I used to complete every broadsheet cryptic crossword by lunchtime, having warmed up on the *Guardian Quick*, while her exposure to mind games was limited to one-sided conversations with a celebrity turning the pages of a dictionary on afternoon TV.

'You mean the *paperboy*, Mr Murray,' she had said. 'He brings you your *newspaper.*'

She had said it with a raised tone of her voice, like I was also deaf, which I wasn't; though I suspect I may be now.

The lad was young and artless. He would expect me to be a stupid old man, because that's the nature of the beasts we are. We play our roles according to where we are in the cycle of life. On this particular day, I hoped he might remind me of the words I had lost without raising his voice or his eyebrows because he had never known me as that other, better man, who used to leave the house with a briefcase and a black-and-white thing under his arm in order to drive to work in the car he owned. He would only know me as the stupid old man who lived at number whatever.

'Wait, son,' I said, beckoning from my partially opened front door.

'Hello?' he replied, turning on my doorstep and wrenching the wires from his head. Good for him—they would have to find someone else for their brain experiment now.

'Remind me, would you,' I said, carefully measuring my words, which I was learning to do in order to secure people's attention long enough for them to register that I may not be the full ticket, and to take pity. 'What is it that you're called? And what's this?' I indicated the roll-up in my hand.

'I'm called Pawel,' said the boy. 'And that's your newspaper.'

Pawel?

Pawel?

What in God's name was that? That was never the word for the person who brought the black-and-white roll-up thing. Not in all my born days.

'What?'

'Pawel,' said the boy, with a smile. 'My parents are from Poland.'

I must have shaken my head at him. Still smiling, he reached for the writer that was sticking out of my dressing gown pocket and wrote the word on the top of my black-and-white, my *newspaper*.

P A W E L

'Pawel!' I replied, awash with enlightenment. '*Polish leader adopts English law and troubled boy.* Answer: *Pawel.* You see?'

'It's just my name,' said the boy with a shrug.

'It's cryptic,' I said. 'But it's logical. You merely break it down to find the answer. Like stripping an engine.'

'I have my bike,' he said. His smile was different from Mrs Grayling's. It conveyed the desire to share information, to divulge; perhaps to sympathise rather than to patronise.

'A bike is a simple engine,' I divulged back.

*

I underwent ECT in the 1960s, when it was a popular treatment for mental breakdown. It is the abbreviation of electroconvulsive therapy. I try not to dwell on it, although I am inclined to misread the abbreviation of *et cetera* as ECT when I am unravelling a puzzle.

This modern world with its advanced gadgetry has also changed its way of dealing with mental illness. Everyone's allowed a little breakdown these days, and the confession of an inability to cope from time to time is positively encouraged. There's a man on daytime TV, whom I've heard ranting through the wall from Mrs Grayling's lounge and subsequently tuned in to myself while waiting for my lunch to be delivered, who appears to be on a mission to drag such confessions out of people. The premise is, I think, that there will be some sort of catharsis and these people will return to their ordered lives. I distrust the man, however, who has a look of the bully-boy about him, and the people seem beyond hope to me. I find myself wondering which came first: their trauma, or their desire to make a public spectacle of it in front of that self-satisfied oaf.

In 1964, there was no ranting man, but there was ECT. If ever there were a sledgehammer to crack a nut. I was an engineer who was capable of diagnosis, deconstruction, repair; I was never cut out to be a manager of men. These men came with welfare problems beyond my frame of reference: wives, families. I wanted no part of their lives, but, having had them foisted upon me, I wanted all of them to prosper. If their doctor saw fit to sign them off for their ailments, who was I to question him? I hadn't earned a brass nameplate next to *my* doorbell. If their wives were having babies during working hours, how could I expect them to be away from their bedside? If they sustained injuries whilst operating dangerous equipment, how could I not bear the brunt of responsibility? I was their *manager*—the buck stopped with me.

The trouble was, I had never sought the buck, and wasn't even aware I was playing a game of poker in the first place. I can explain that 'passing the buck' is a term derived from the buckhorn handle of the knife which indicates your turn to deal at cards. I know this on days when I don't know what the boy Pawel is called, which is confounding, but reminds me, maddeningly, that my brain isn't quite ready for decommissioning yet.

In 1964 I shut down.

I sat in the corner of my kitchen until Alf from Head Office came banging on my door in his three piece charcoal suit and miasma of *Old Spice*.

We chatted man to man, although I may have wept at one point. I remember coming off my bicycle as a boy and tearing up my shins so badly that my brother's friend, Big Doug, had to carry me home. Big Doug wasn't blessed with the smarts but he had the strength of an ox and wouldn't leave our house until my mother told him I would be as right as rain after an iodine wash and a suck of a barley sugar sweet. From that day forward, whenever Doug saw me he would wax lyrical about my bravery. He never once mentioned that I cried like a girl all the way home.

Alf arranged for me to see a good 'head doctor' and the shocking of my brain began. I put myself in his hands as I was out of control. Alf appeared to be a better manager of men than I was, as he was taking charge of my welfare. He stopped the buck.

It is only now old age has brought some serenity in the form of self-knowledge (together with the onset of madness) that I realise Alf managed me rather badly. He died not long ago. His wife sent the customary Christmas card with a note saying that he had not survived a heart bypass operation. Lucky Alf.

My memory was never the same after 1964. I can still picture all four of the Beatles, but by the time they were releasing albums separately and sniping at each other I could not remember any of their names. But this was hardly debilitating. I got by and continued to keep my wits sharp with my work and my daily crossword puzzles.

I'm not permitted to blame Alf or ECT. Indeed, my own father lost his memory and I think *his* father did before him. I'm sure they took it in their stride; as blissfully ignorant as babies, which is how I recall the evening of my dad's life experience to be—although not so blissful for my mother and my sisters who had to take care of him.

As for me, I have been watching at the door of the workshop since 1964 for signs of deterioration in my engine. I could have started plotting a graph with the subtlest of downward curves which ends at the point where I am today, in the year two-thousand-and-something, at my minimum point; my *nadir*. There has been no control study to show that the electricity they shot through my brain had no bearing whatsoever on the miserable outcome of my life.

I bitterly resent Alf for his cunning interpretation of the compound noun 'bypass'. There will be no systematic deterioration, degradation, or decommissioning for him. He bypassed all of it.

*

I wake to the sound of his bicycle hitting my gate. It's a struggle but I am determined to make it to the door. I have a feeling this will be the best part of my day.

Pawel.

I have written his name on the whiteboard that one of the carers put up in my kitchen, copied from the top of the paper where he wrote it down for me. It is, in fact, the first word I have written up there.

It is Tuesday. This means I also have plum crumble to look forward to when the lunch lady comes: plum crumble with Carnation milk. I would rather be dead, though. When the next Tuesday comes around, I may well have forgotten what plum crumble is.

Pawel. I repeat it like it is part of an instruction.

'You're always in your pyjamas,' he says to me, liberated from his wires.

'Yes,' I reply. This latest information is confusing.

*

Another day, I am watching from my window. His mouth is moving to the song in his head and he is pushing at his nose with the back of his wrist.

'I have something for you, Mr Murray.' He hands me a shirt: crumpled, with dangling arms. 'It's for during the day.'

I look into his youthful face, the contours uncreased by age but blighted by several spots and dirty pores. He should keep his hands cleaner, I think, which presents me with the notion of *Swarfega.* No matter how filthy my working day had been, I always returned home with clean hands and fingernails.

'Did your mother send this?' I ask.

'No way,' says Pawel. 'Don't tell her, she'd have a fit. I took it from someone's recycling bag. Technically it isn't stealing.'

I turn the shirt around my hand and think of the plastic bags I had filled with china and old books with the help of one of the carers. These were things I no longer used. I contemplate Pawel's logic and admire it.

'Thank you,' I say.

*

I had put the shirt on over my pyjamas. It was a tight fit. Pawel came into the hall this time, his wires loose about his neck, and unbuttoned both the shirt and my pyjama top, stripping me to my vest, before fastening the shirt back on me. It fitted better, although I was left with the quandary of holding a spare shirt.

'Put that in the washer,' he said.

'OK,' I replied. I pointed my shirtless hand at his wires. 'You aren't plugged in.'

'Not at the moment.'

He grinned and put the plug ends back into his ears.

'I can't hear what you're saying,' I said, feeling agitated. I reached out and tugged at one of the wires. I feared I may have been a bit rough, and anticipated a rebuke such as the one I often received from a carer when he or she was trying to help me (with my slippers, for example) and when I responded with a spiteful snatch. Sometimes spite cracked out of me like firing a cap gun: sudden but harmless.

Pawel removed the other wire between print-smudged fingers and said, 'You don't mean that, Mr Murray. You mean *I* can't hear what *you're* saying.'

His words were out there with mine, and I understood.

*

I never had a wife. I would have been an intolerable man

to live with and hate making idle conversation. If you aren't a crossword puzzler, you don't understand the imperative to solve. You solve and feel resolved. Shopping for household items or hanging curtains are simply irrelevant and trivial pursuits in comparison: solving nothing.

My abilities are diminishing. To be erudite—a fine and lamentably overlooked word—is everything; and I am reduced to one broadsheet a day, delivered by Pawel, the *paperboy*. It is *The Daily Telegraph,* which does me no discredit, but it is the last vestige of my honour. I await the co-related answers to the first two horizontal clues in the small puzzle to be *Death,* and then *Nell* (clue: *Gwynne, perhaps*), so that I can write them in with my Biro and accept them as a portent.

*

'Am I for your lessons?' I ask him, on a day when I have arranged for the carer to leave us out some cakes: *Mr Kipling's Fondant Fancies.*

'You are nothing to do with my school,' says Pawel. He winces as he bites into one of the pink cakes which are very sweet and will dissolve into your cavities (if you have any) like battery acid. I am smug about my dentures.

'I thought you might be here for your lessons.' I mean something more than lessons, something other than school, but the concept and the words are at odds with each other.

'I don't do any projects outside of school, Mr Murray. Except to teach Polish to local people, with my parents.'

'Your father,' I say, remembering some snippet of our recent history—mine and Pawel's. 'Did he have a bad time in the war?'

Pawel grins and moves his shoulders up and down.

'There is no war,' he says, leaving his plate and half his cake. 'There hasn't been a war for a long time.'

*

I remember my brother Ed saying that Elvis and *rock 'n' roll* was the start of the rot, music-wise. But it's a matter of opinion. I have always preferred classical music, because it allows you to confer your own sense of meaning, without the insolence of someone else's usually oversentimental lyrics. I like the frowning German with the wild hair; more and more I like him as I sink into sympathetic deafness.

Pawel puts his music into my head, like fitting hearing aids, so that I will stop fussing about his wires. It helps.

At first it is a cacophony, then it finds its equilibrium between my ears and I begin to glean a pattern out of the mayhem. Layer upon layer of sound arrives and settles like the sheet, the blanket, the eiderdown, gradually building to the complete and comfortable status of an overture. It isn't *Beethoven,* the wild-haired German, but it is something new and extraordinary. It is someone's craft.

I tap the knees of my pyjamas.

Pawel laughs and taps along with me. He laughs and taps and sometimes he keeps one of the wire plugs to himself, and we are listening to the same sound with different ears.

*

The woman next door keeps bringing me my *Daily Telegraph* without Pawel. She includes a paperback book of crosswords which I tell my carer can go in the bag where Pawel found my shirt. I have no use for such a thing: crosswords don't belong in books, unless they are put together for dim-witted people going on long coach journeys who don't normally do crosswords.

I meet his mother. She has his same small, dark eyes like currants pushed into raw pastry; no spots, but an unfortunate smattering of hairs on her upper lip. She talks with Mrs Grayling and they clutch their hands anxiously together—women who make buns, hang curtains, watch television in the daytime.

I know I must stop asking about Pawel because it is a tedious question for the carers. Michael is the most tolerant about my slippers, and he sits on the bed with me and explains that the boy is dead: killed by a speeding car.

My first thought is that I scarcely need *The Daily Telegraph* anymore, anyway, as on most days I can't fill all the squares.

*

I wake to the sound of his bicycle at my gate, only this time it's not his bicycle at all, but the woman's with the currant eyes, here at the same time as the carer. They make hot drinks for three people.

The new woman takes white wires out of her handbag, unwinding them so she can plug the ends into my ears. I am cheerful as she and the carer grip each other and shed tears, like the scene with Mrs Grayling.

Pawel's music fills my head with the stuff of our lives: his, and mine.

'What day is it today?' I ask.

They are alarmed because I am shouting.

'It's Tuesday,' mouths Pawel's mother.

It will be plum crumble, then, I think. I tap my fingers on the knees of my pyjamas.

'Good!' I shout at the carers. Their eyes hold messages that are about more than me and my lunch. I start to wonder what became of Pawel; and John, Paul, George and Ringo.

The Spirit of Maura Molloy

'Every abuser of a body or a mind should pause for thought if her sandwich tastes funny or his beer smells off'

CARRIE SPLASHED HER FACE WITH WATER AND DARED TO look in the mirror. It was the worst yet. Her left eye was swollen like a rotten apple that was ready to split open and spew out maggots that would feast on her tainted flesh.

She could just about make herself out, the essence of herself, in her good eye. She mouthed the words *I hate you* and went downstairs to make his breakfast.

'You've made that worse,' he said, scraping eggs, bacon and mushrooms around his plate and swilling them down his throat with gulps of tea.

She calmly shook her head at him. She had two days before the start of term. A new term at a new school in a new town. It was the pattern of their lives—hers, Eddie's and Victoria's—move in, mess up, and move on.

The bruises were usually fairly easy to disguise (even throttle marks could be gagged under a bright scarf) but this one would take some explaining. Her inventions to cover up the appalling truth could be as colourful as her hidden flesh—falling furniture, a collapsed exercise bike, brittle bones—although she had a feeling the new headmistress at St Peter's was going to be neither gullible nor insensitive enough to let too many injuries go unnoticed. Clearly, they would be moving on from this town sooner than usual.

Staring at her beleaguered reflection in the bathroom mirror, the prospect of uprooting her daughter from yet another new school, in the middle of A Levels, hit her like a second invisible body blow.

Victoria appeared for breakfast in her customary black garb, her dark hair newly dyed and straightened to make her look like a glossy, funereal raven. She took in her mum's battered face without flinching, and reached for the Cheerios.

'Are you going out like that?' Eddie sneered. Vicky glanced down at herself briefly, at her black leggings that revealed the contours of her athletic legs and her oversized black vest adorned with a large glittering cross. She ignored him.

'You'll never get a boyfriend dressed like that. You don't even look like a woman. And what's the cross about? Are you the fucking Virgin Mary?'

They persisted with their silent, tasteless breakfast until they heard the door bang behind him.

'I swear to God, one day I'll kill him.'

'This, seriously, was my fault...'

'Shut *up*, Mum!'

Carrie stopped, conceding she was about to talk nonsense. Vicky was sixteen years old—beautiful, intelligent and sensitive. She deserved more than her mother's hopeless lies. She would reserve them for her colleagues, the neighbours, the doctors.

One day she would find courage, and her first act of bravery would be to tell Victoria that Eddie was not her father. That life was different twenty years ago—in her grandparents' house at least—when falling pregnant in your teens was terribly shaming. That Granny and Granddad weren't bad people, that Eddie was prepared to marry her despite her condition and presented as an honourable man. They weren't to know that the affable fellow who enjoyed a port and lemon with them in the pub, and called their daughter his 'hen', would go on to drink another ten pints of beer when they'd gone, and kick and punch his whore of a wife all the way home.

Vicky was a different girl from her mother at sixteen: bright and resourceful, she would take no stick from anyone. But she had grown up casting herself in the role of her mother's protector—'if he comes near me, I'll stab him'—which made Carrie's heart shrink at her own lack of resolve and the looming fear of how life would end up for both of them when Vicky left for university. Carrie's only source of pride and purpose in life was her daughter, and how she was turning out, against the odds. She had faced a new school and repeated rounds of the same difficult questions half a dozen times in her young life, but she had met each challenge with extraordinary aplomb, as though she were able to recharge her own strength from her mother's adversity. Of course she wanted to be free of her tyrannical father as much as Carrie did, but she understood there was no easy route away from him for either of them.

'You're going to have to do something about that eye,' she said, sensibly. 'Get out of the house for a bit. I will do some more of the project for you.'

Carrie was preparing for her Year 4s by investigating local heroes of the past and present. The project refined the children's research skills and they enjoyed the sense of celebrity that was often at the heart of their entertainment these days. The thought of their eager faces (even their sulky ones) raised her spirits; and the safety of her outside world, which was always preferable to the chaos of her inner one, gave her a glimmer of hope that, maybe this time, everything would be alright.

She walked to the local park, which appeared to be part of the grounds of an old manor house. The air was fresh with the promise of impending autumn, but the sky remained summer blue and there was an uplifting fragrance of roses. She sat on a bench with her bag of potions from *Boots* and watched a squirrel scamper up a tree trunk like a helter-skelter in reverse. For a moment she closed her eyes on her troubles and basked in the warmth. This was a lovely place: perhaps it would become her sanctuary for as long as she would be able to live there.

Carrie opened her eyes at the rustling of her plastic bag. For a moment she thought it was the inquisitive squirrel, then she realised she was letting her reverie get the better of her as it was a young woman taking a seat on the bench beside her.

'You've got quite a shiner, there,' the woman said, with an Irish lilt. 'What's the excuse this time, stepped on a rake?'

Carrie was brought unhappily to her senses and gathered her bags protectively closer.

'I am the clumsiest person in the world,' she said, feeling she owed a stranger no explanation of her circumstances.

'What's in the bag?' the woman asked. She was certainly forward. She moved uncomfortably close, her ink-blue eyes assessing Carrie all over from under tousled bleached-blonde hair. She must have been a couple of years older than Vicky, with the same taste in what Eddie called 'dykey' clothes. She had a tattooed forearm and a black belt covered in blunt spikes, but smelled extraordinarily feminine as though the perfume of the roses had intensified on her arrival.

'Bits and pieces. Make-up,' said Carrie. She shuffled to the edge of her seat in readiness to go.

'He beats you up, love, don't he?' said the stranger, in a matter-of-fact way as Carrie got to her feet. 'I could tell even without the bruises.'

Carrie froze, her back to the woman. She wasn't completely cowardly or lost to reason. She had tried a women's refuge when Vicky was small; she had been to self-help groups. But for as long as he was out there with those fists and that need to drink and rage at an easy target, she knew there was no reliable means of escape.

'Has he started on your daughter yet?'

'How dare you!' said Carrie, welling up with the practised indignance of a teacher. 'I came here for some fresh air and peace and quiet…'

'Not in *my* rose garden, Mrs,' said the stranger with a mischievous smile. She sat back with her arms wide, wrists dangling, and one ankle over her knee, displaying the powerful tread of her boot. A kick from those boots would do some damage, Carrie imagined, with a surge of strange satisfaction. Vicky had a similar pair.

Carrie looked around in amusement.

'This is *not* your rose garden,' she said pleasantly.

'But it's beautiful, ain't it?' the stranger replied. 'I'm Maura. Not originally from round these parts, but I reckon I've been here longer than you. Have you seen the forest?'

'The ancient Savernake Forest,' said Carrie cheerfully, regaining her seat and dismissing gloomy thoughts. 'I've read about it. A great favourite of Henry the Eighth. It's on my list.'

'Of things to see before you *leave*?' Maura's chin tilted impishly in her direction.

Discomfort curdled Carrie's insides.

'Yes,' she said.

'Well, then. Allow me to be your escort!'

Carrie entertained the notion that it was foolish to follow a stranger into the woods, then reminded herself, as her pace quickened beside that of Maura Somebody, that the greatest danger in her life remained what was behind her closed doors at home every night. She thought of Vicky giggling with complicit glee at her mother's abandon.

The forest was lively with picnicking families making the most of their freedom before the start of the school term. Carrie felt a familiar prick of envy at how other people lived. Eddie would never have accompanied them on a family camping trip, or allowed them the freedom to venture out alone. Campsites were too far from pubs, and too public to enable him to visit his private, unpleasant acts upon her.

Maura cut a familiar path through the holiday traffic of the forest and they found themselves in the cool privacy of tall, majestic trees where even the birdsong seemed muted out of respect for the sanctity of the spot. There was the occasional scampering of a grey squirrel or the crackle of undergrowth where the women were stepping, but they were otherwise in a haven of solitude.

'This is splendid, Maura,' said Carrie, blissfully. 'It's just what I needed today.'

Maura busied herself around the roots of the trees and began to fill Carrie's *Boots* bag with handfuls of mushrooms.

'Perfectly edible,' she said, briskly, seeing Carrie's look of mild horror. Maura turned the specimens over in Carrie's palm to show her how to identify their safety from the colour of their gills and the shape of their roots. Her fingers were thick from outdoor work, their lines etched with dirt. 'Trust me. My brothers and sisters and I used to live off these.'

'My goodness, in this day and age?'

Maura fixed her with her challenging blue eyes as she wiped the soil from her hands onto her black jeans.

'Oh aye, love. You'd be surprised how some people live.'

'I didn't mean to offend you,' said Carrie.

'I'm not offended, Mrs,' said Maura, glibly. 'A few words thrown at me never did me any harm.'

'Do you work here, have family?'

'I work here when I'm needed. My family has moved on.'

'Oh. I can rather relate to that.'

Maura shook her head in smiling contradiction.

'I just meant their time had come, love.'

*

They eventually returned to the main road and Maura showed Carrie the bus stop where she could get back home most expediently. Three hours had gone by since she had left Vicky at work at the kitchen table; she hadn't even begun to think about Eddie's laundry or their supper.

 'Maybe I'll see y'around,' the young Irish woman chirped as they took their leave of each other. 'The forest isn't as big as you might think.'

 'That would be nice,' said Carrie, by way of a farewell, but watched the bold young woman stride away from her in her ragged denim waistcoat and biker boots in the knowledge that they were from very different worlds and were unlikely to ever cross paths again.

*

Carrie made the two of them a late lunch of mushroom omelette.

 'Mmm, these are good,' said Vicky. 'Where did you get them? Not Tesco's, I bet, 'cos they were covered in crap.'

 'No,' said her mother, casting a look of mild reproach. 'I picked them myself. I am learning what to look for.'

*

She dabbed at her eye before he came home and did some repair work with the heavy foundation the lady had recommended in the chemist, in the hope it would appease him.

Vicky was playing her music loudly in her room and talking to her new friend Olivia on her phone. She would no doubt be keeping one eye on the window so that she would be able to turn down and ring off before her father walked in.

Carrie made him a steak dinner on his return: it was Monday, so it was what he would expect. Vicky was hovering to talk to her mum about the research work she had done on her behalf earlier that day, but preferred to wait until he had finished shovelling his food and gone out to the pub.

 'Have you two done anything useful today?' Eddie said. He cracked open a can at the table, and dirty froth spurted out to emphasise his disdain.

 'Prepping for school, mostly,' said Vicky. 'And you?'

Carrie winced at her daughter's impertinent tone.

 'The usual shite to put food on the table,' he grunted.

While the two women were making a shared unspoken note that it was *Carrie* who had put some of the food—the mushrooms—on the table that day, they observed Eddie cramming a forkful of meat, chips and fungi into his mouth as one might watch garbage tumbling into a landfill site. He choked briefly—the *pig*, thought Vicky—and dropped his cutlery, allowing the food to fall from his mouth onto his plate.

'What the fuck?' he said. Eddie put his hands to his throat and stood up, his chair scraping back with a sound like the blare of distressed cattle. He gave an almighty groan and fell back into his seat, his head cracking forward onto the table, hitting his fork like the down stroke of a seesaw and sending it flying across the room.

'We've killed him!' shrieked Victoria, her eyes wild with horrified delight.

'*He's not your father!*' Carrie shouted at her and sank down onto the chair beside him.

*

The policewoman was the personification of kindly, understated professionalism. Carrie and Vicky were taken away from the house for questioning, in two separate rooms, at the local police station.

Victoria caught her mum's eye for a moment as they went their divided ways.

'I think the police force could be for me, you know,' she said. 'Bloody love the uniform.'

Carrie sat with her head bowed forward. A male police officer had joined them.

'And you can't think of anything else your husband said about what might have happened to him before he got home today?' he asked.

'I've told you everything,' she replied. 'It was the mushrooms. It's my fault. I've killed him.'

The officers exchanged generous glances.

'But you all ate these mushrooms, love,' said the woman. 'There will need to be a toxicology report, of course, but the initial impression seems to be that your husband died of an unrelated heart condition. You are clearly very distressed.'

Carrie looked up sharply. She couldn't remember a time when she had felt less distressed.

The police officers left her for a few moments, one saying under her breath to the other, 'By the look of that black eye, maybe she's had a lucky escape.'

*

Carrie was sitting at her kitchen table the next day with a mug of tea. It was no longer a crime scene, although she noticed Eddie's fork was still under the butcher's block. What an oversight—another example of how overstretched the police force was, which was perhaps why it didn't always have time for calls about domestic violence. Vicky had only called them once when she was around eight years old. No one came.

Her daughter appeared in her dressing gown. With her dark make up removed she looked like a little girl again.

'Are you up for talking 'project'?' she asked, waggling a brown manila envelope. 'I mean, life goes on...'

'Of course,' said Carrie. 'It does.'

'You are *so* going to love this!' said Vicky, conspiratorially pulling up a chair and casting off her forced sense of mourning. 'It's the best local story yet, although you might have to do some work on it for your precious Year 4s as it's about *the love that dare not speak its name*!'

'Oh,' said Carrie, with a wry smile. 'Just up your street, then.'

'You bet! Listen!' Vicky drew out the papers that she had printed off at the library and tucked her hair behind her ears. 'It's the story of Maura Molloy. Do they mean *Maura*? I've never heard that name before.'

'I think it may be Irish.' Carrie felt blood rising to prick her ears with curiosity.

'That explains it. Maura Molloy was a girl who came over here from Ireland in the 1860s. She was from a large but poor family who all ended up in service. Maura worked at the old Manor as a kitchen girl-cum-gardener. Apparently she fell in love with the lady of the house and they began a passionate, clandestine affair. Lord Robert, as the story goes, was a bit of a tyrant by nature—not like his gentle and well-respected Mrs—so, of course, when he found out he wasn't best pleased. He didn't send Maura away, but used to beat her up regularly, along with Lady Constance, whilst getting them both to do his sexual bidding...'

'Oh Vic, doesn't that sound a bit far-fetched,' said Carrie, her heart thrilling slightly in her chest. 'How can that much *intimate* detail be known about these people?'

'Dunno, but it's all there on the internet. The Lord was so unpopular, by all accounts, that the rest of the household used to help keep Constance and Maura's assignations under wraps, and, when he died, Maura sort of became her consort which I assume means they were at it out in the open, at last. Maura was promoted to head gardener— there is even a local rose named after her—and they kind of lived happily ever after.

'The *best* part, though, is that she is supposed to haunt the grounds of the old Manor—there have been sightings of her by both night and day. *And*, although Lord Robert was certified as having died from natural causes, there was talk that she and the Lady and the kitchen staff gradually poisoned him with stuff they were growing in the garden! It fell into common parlance for a while that if a man died in unusual circumstances he was said to have had 'a visit from Maura Molloy'!'

Vicky paused as though she wanted to say something pertinent, and wickedly cutting, about Eddie, but thought better of it.

'Well, well. I'm sure I can sanitise it for my Year 4s. What a story.'

Carrie's eyes softened at her daughter. 'I guess I have a story for *you*, too, about your real dad. I'm so sorry I've not been straight with you, Vicky…'

'But not tonight, Mum,' said Victoria, rubbing her eyes with the back of her hand. 'I want to think about our *future* for now, not our past. Can I invite Livvy round for tea tomorrow? She's going to be in my English class and she seems to, you know, *get* me.'

'Of course,' said Carrie. She felt undeniably numb, but would wait for her daughter to take herself off to bed so she could rifle through her paperwork with unguarded delight, and smile at the grainy pictures of Maura Molloy's feisty, arrogant features under her baker-boy flat cap or clad in her gardening apron.

'She's vegetarian like me, too,' added Vicky, planting a kiss on the top of her mum's head.

'Right-o,' said Carrie. 'Perhaps I'll pick us some more mushrooms.'

Learning to Love Spiders

For those who tread water in the wake of
someone else's grief

CHARLOTTE A. CAVATICA.

It was such a beautiful, important name.

It could have been the name of the first woman to be the president of America or the real name of a cool singer like Lady Gaga.

It could have been *your* name, Charlotte, because *you* are beautiful and important. To me.

I didn't think it should have been the name of a spider. Unbeautiful little creatures that they are… well, they *are* little compared to a dog or a bus; but they are big and terrifying in the imagination of a six-year-old girl with a ten-year-old brother who liked to startle and upset her by putting spiders in her bed and down the back of her top.

Charlotte (story Charlotte) was a spider in my schoolbook, and we were supposed to like her, although I could only ever like the pig.

The pig was easy to love. He was cute and cuddly with a person-like face, and no one wanted *him* to die. Spiders die all the time. If you cover them with cups or washed-out yoghurt pots they die in a couple of days. Sometimes they look like they are still alive and ready to pounce on you; other times they are all curled up, their spirits already gone off to spider heaven.

47

My brother died covered up. I took the bed sheet off him because I thought he might have been like a spider that seems dead but isn't, but my mum kept telling me not to do that. First nicely and then all angry, with tears messing up her face—the tears she cried whenever she glass-tested my skin to see if I had the same sort of spots that were on Davey when he died.

I didn't see any spiders for a while after that, maybe because Davey had brought them all to me and, with him gone, they weren't that bothered with a silly little girl like his scaredy-cat left-behind baby sister anymore. I mean, they wouldn't *choose* to go down the back of my dress without him, would they?

I wanted a day back, just one day, when Davey's fingers, his hand, his arm, were on the other end of the tickling terror down the back of my sweater, when my eyes were tight shut against *The Invasion of the Spider from Space* with its snapping jaws and hairy legs. There would be screaming and a telling-off for both of us, but by teatime he would still be there in his seat, and Mum's scowl would actually mean she was happier than she is today, when her best smile is just a straight line.

Then a spider came back one evening when I was in bed. It was being lowered from the ceiling on an invisible thread and it stopped, inches from my nose, where it had a good look at me before deciding whether or not it was going to kill me. It made busy movements with its front legs like a butcher sharpening his knives.

Suddenly it didn't matter to me and I wasn't afraid. I was outside of myself looking down onto a small thing versus a big one. One of us was David and the other was Goliath. I thought that if Davey wouldn't be afraid, why should I be? The worst thing that could happen was that it would kill me—which would be quick, at least, because of all the spider poison—and then I would see him again, in *real* heaven.

Davey in heaven is one of my best thoughts, after my thoughts of you, Charlotte.

It is a place he would have been surprised to find himself in at first because our Sunday school teacher, Miss Grinyer, always said 'you two will never get to heaven' when we took extra squash. Our places in heaven were always hit-and-miss because of taking extra squash and other things that offended the Lord, but my mum sends her prayers there, so it must be where he ended up.

I like to think of him as he always was, alive with mischief in a heavenly garden where there are no borders to trample and where the girl angels won't think unforgivable things about him for putting spiders down their necks.

*

I still keep spiders under yoghurt pots, but they are my pets. My friends.

Here are some things I've learned about spiders:

One. Spiders are not partial to solid food. In fact, a spider only eats liquid food, which suits her very well indeed and she thrives and survives on this and doesn't get any grief from other members of the creepy-crawly kingdom for the life choice she has made. She may look spindly in a certain light and in need of a good square meal, but give her a job to do like making a brilliant new web (which she does every day) and she will find the energy. I suppose she decides what's worth fighting for, and when she's done she can choose to hang like a spent thing with no interest in what's going on in the rest of the world around her until she's ready to spin (or suck her lunch) again.

That's the thing about a spider, she is her own woman. Like you, my strong and spindly Charlotte.

Two. Spiders are programmed not to worry too much about their brothers. Or their sisters, for that matter. They are born with lots, so that if one brother gets squashed, or covered in deadly spots, and dies, there is another one (or two, or three, or four or… *hundreds*) to take his place. The life of a spider sister is very straightforward, and never lonely; and the life of a spider mum is not described as *not worth living, not anymore, without him* if she loses one of her spider children, because she is busy spinning her heart out to catch flies for the living ones.

Three. A spider knows how to deal with an annoying man.

Davey used to say rhymes like 'boys are it and girls are shit' but he would stand between me and the worst of the name callers and the chewing-gum-in-my-hair-stickers at school. I don't think he would have grown up to be as bad as the boys who were scattered around *you*, Charlotte, like the crusts off your sandwiches—crusts that even *I* wouldn't eat for you, if you begged me, because they were dry and dull, and would have tasted of nothing but disappointment. A spider has to have a mate from time to time. It seems it's just the way things are; otherwise there would be no brave Daveys, no beautiful Charlottes and no dumb Daisys in the world. But the cleverest thing a spider does, I think, is to do sex with a mate and then put him in the blender for tea.

*

I have a spider in the room with me today. She is tiger-striped and quite amazing: she travels about the kitchen on a zip wire. I think she is interested in my cake, which is cut into two pieces. One for me and one for you.

I won't let you down, though, Charlotte. I will eat both pieces.

Come to think of it, the boys called you 'spider girl' when you came back from your holiday abroad with your legs turned brown and your hair in all those dreadlocks; and I thought *ha!* because that was what I might have called you if I had had a longer time to think about it. But not in a nasty voice, like they did.

They preferred you when you had bigger boobs, because boys are like that, but I love you better the way you are now. You like your bones better than your boobs, so *I* do too. Besides, if you were a spider, I reckon big boobs would get in the way of your zipping and web building.

The boys made love bruises on your neck when they still fancied you. I noticed them when we were in the girls' loos and I held your bag for you because you didn't want it putting down on the dirty wet floor.

'Shit, Daisy, how will he ever fancy me if I look like the side of a house?' you said.

'Why should he fancy you anyway?' I thought. I still think that. He was our teacher: it wasn't his job to fancy you. The boys fancying you was bad enough.

Also, the side of my house is fairly massive, but not much bigger than the house from any other angle. And nowhere *near* as lovely as you. Because you *are* lovely, Charlotte. Your skin is the best; your hair does blonde and dark in all the right places. Every fashionable thing looks good on you. I would hold your bag out of the wee on the loo floor for forever and a day if you asked me to.

I told you that being sick is the easiest peasiest thing in the world: you stick your fingers down your throat and hello again macaroni cheese with sausage pieces. Hey presto, you get to stay at home with your mum's eyes on you all day.

It made you *feel* sick, but not enough to *do* sick. So you took some of those tablets that make you poo. I was sad that my clever sicking up trick didn't work on you, but I was happy that we spent most of our lunchtime together, and you said a kind thing to me along the lines of 'it's not nice that everyone calls you Crazy Daisy' while you watched me eat up all our crisps and Babybels and chocolate bars on the school steps, away from everyone.

*

I am going to write the next time I can visit you on my calendar.

The first time I came to see you was the best, because you were very funny about how you were going to hide your food, and we were like the wizard girls who share dorms in Harry Potter, planning adventures. You let me use the hair straighteners on you, and *he* wasn't around, creeping about like Creeping Jesus (as my Nan would say) and neither were any other girls from school because they had all stopped liking you by then, same as the boys. It was how I always dreamed it would be: just me and you behind a door we could lock if we wanted to.

The second time was the worst because you had a tube in your nose and you didn't laugh when I opened my bag and poured your soup into it.

The other times get mixed up in my head. I hate it when I turn up and he's there and you let him stay but I can't. I don't understand that about you, Charlotte. He is not a proper friend to you: he never brings a bag for the food with him, for a start.

Today's spider is interested in our cake. Maybe the chocolate pieces remind her of flies.

I wrote on my calendar the next time I could visit you but my mum rubbed it off. Luckily we do appointments in pencil, but I get really cross when things change about. It was on there for days, and then she had a phone call and rubbed it off, just like that.

'Charlotte isn't well enough for visits, anymore', she said, but I think that's a lie—I can hear a lie in people's voices, like 'Charlotte's only using you, you stupid bitch' or 'I have to see Charlotte to talk about her maths'. You didn't like maths, you only liked wasting our precious time with the maths teacher.

*

No matter how much you hate spiders and brothers, you don't *actually* want them to die, even if you sometimes think it really hard.

Maybe *he* will die now, Creeping Jesus, like Davey did, under a sheet. Or a really big yoghurt pot.

Now my spider is hanging like a person on a trapeze at the circus waiting for us to clap. This can also mean she's dead, Charlotte.

We'll have to wait and see.

Come Together

'The turning of a worm might result in an
earthquake'

SHE RUSHED INTO HER HOUSE LIKE SOMEBODY WHO WAS about to throw up or defecate. However, Clare had no urge to do either, just to slam the door behind her and to breathe through the moment. To pant, almost, like a dog.

There was a dead man upstairs in her bed but Tilly had needed her walk. She was a crazy little spaniel cross who may have had a psychological disorder so it never felt right to break her routine. She would be calm now for a while, so Clare hung up her lead and sprinted noiselessly up to the bedroom.

There he remained, as pale as unfired clay, with his cheek pressed into her pillow in mock-slumber.

Had he not resembled
My father as he slept, I had done't

Only she hadn't done it. He had done it himself; or, at least, it had happened all on its own.

They had shared her gazpacho (*yes, chilled*, she had insisted at the sight of his quizzical expression, *like it's supposed to be!*) followed by Tournados Rossini and poached pears. A perfect meal, even if she said so herself. She couldn't have been more pleased with how it turned out. But with the talk of her kitchen endeavours swiftly dispensed with, she had felt the evening begin to slip away from her like she had been turned and pushed in a game of blind man's buff. He was steering her towards having sex with him. Not in a coercive way, but by helping himself to her every response of 'yes' or 'I suppose so'—just like he had helped himself to the homemade bread and butter—as a means of confirming that they were both after the same thing.

They *had* been after the same thing, in essence. Only not like this. *Not like this,* she heard a small voice from somewhere near her solar plexus pleading as she stripped down to the pretty new underwear that he wasn't even looking at. She turned cold and quiet while he rattled on about the merits of the flavoured condom. Then he seized his own arm and his chest and then he was dead.

*

Dan knocked on her door at one in the morning. She lurched from what must have been a rigid state of sub-slumber and fastened herself quickly into her dressing gown.

 'I was worried. Your lights are on, I could hear Tilly barking.'

Dan was a terrifying gentleman. *Gentle*-man. He had a bald head and a gravelly voice and teeth engraved with nicotine. How did you trust a man like that? He was her kindest neighbour: he looked out for all the old people and for Clare, because she was on her own. He brought her bin up, mended things. He didn't pry. She had never even made him a cup of tea.

'Dan. Something has happened…'

Her kitchen table was a chessboard of foreplay: the pepper grinder on its side like the toppled, intoxicated king in the midst of the dinner party debris. Dan's small, menacing eyes ran over it and then over her.

'What's happened? Have you been hurt?'

He was a man who would have appreciated Tournados Rossini, she decided. Really appreciated it. She imagined he might show some humility at the sight of a woman's new underwear. She gripped the back of a kitchen chair.

'No, I'm fine, Dan.' Her smile became a grimace of embarrassment. 'Can I get you a cup of tea?'

'Are you on your own?' he asked in some confusion.

'I'm always on my own,' she replied.

'Then I'll have a tea,' he said, squatting rather like a bulldog next to Tilly and fiercely massaging her frayed red ears.

*

'He's died on me, Tessa.'

Tessa was round within the hour, wearing overkill sunglasses and sporting her Chihuahua, Gaga, under her arm. She deposited her scrap of a dog next to Tilly in the big-enough-for-two basket where they were accustomed to tolerating each other, and joined Clare at the dead man's bedside.

'What have you done? Who have you phoned?'

'No one. Dan came round and I made him tea.'

Tessa wrapped her fringed suede arms around her body.

'*Tea?* Are you insane? A man's had a heart attack and died in your bed and you're making tea for Desperate Dan?!'

'I know. A married man, Tessa! I never wanted a married man.'

'Jeez, Louise, you are the fussiest mare I have ever come across. You are never going to get a Mr Darcy at your age. And not with *that* haircut.'

She produced a cigarette and blew smoke at her.

'You know I don't like smoking in my bedroom.'

Tessa had always been able to raise one eyebrow into a perfect arch to punctuate her disdain.

'It will hide the smell of death,' she said, deliberately.

*

'Tell me about him,' said Clare, as they drove out of the village in Tessa's jeep.

'Married, horny, what else do you need to know?'

'Why him, for me?'

Tessa cast her a sideways glance that read like sarcasm veiled, all too thinly, in pity.

''Cos he was up for it. And had the cash,' she said. 'And, for Christ's sake, Clare, virgins over forty like you are like the bits of meat you find rattling around at the bottom of your freezer, stuck all over with peas.' She lifted her fingers off the steering wheel and wiggled them in distaste. '*Not* particularly appetising, love. No disrespect.'

Clare opened her mouth to protest but resorted to shaking her head and sinking her chin into her chest.

'Besides, you should know more about him than me. Didn't the two of you talk over your show-off dinner, before the sight of your dodgy bikini wax gave him a heart attack?'

'Not about anything memorable,' said Clare. She took a careful intake of breath. 'Had you told him, then, about me?'

'What, that he would need power tools and protective goggles to make it past your hymen?'

At this, Tessa beamed at her and squeezed her leg. It was a gesture Clare knew of old that meant she didn't totally despise her in spite of her cruel words: that she probably considered Clare her best friend, her only friend. She who had been pleasuring boys and men since the age of fifteen and who remained on a kind of mission to get Clare penetrated by somebody, *anybody,* before they were both killed by separate but related conditions of frustration.

Tessa's mission had accompanied them from high school through first-class degrees in English Literature at the same university, where Clare was often kept waiting outside a bedroom or a toilet door while her best friend made noises of pseudo-operatic climax before she joined her for a lit cigarette and her next coat of lipstick.

'You faked that one,' Clare once said, crossly. 'I can tell, you know. You start sort of *rhyming.*'

*

Tessa pulled into a truck-stop-cum-café. It was exactly the sort of testosterone-soused venue that made Clare's sexual confidence shrink like a snail into its shell; or, like one of Tessa's fabled withered male appendages, back into its foreskin.

'He simply couldn't get it up. I swear to God it was like sitting on a thimble.'

They ordered cups of coffee and examined the big, brazen face of the truck-stop clock.

'Give it an hour and it will be getting dark,' said Tessa, briskly. 'Two rounds of coffee should do it.'

At quarter past the hour, a man pulled up outside in a pick-up and had barely removed his sunglasses and begun strolling across the forecourt when Clare had slipped out and pushed the bin bag of the dead man's belongings under the tarpaulin of his truck. She peeled off her gloves and dropped them secretively into the water bucket. She had seen screen sirens remove their gloves in a similar way, in the act of seduction. She was back with Tessa sipping their coffee by the time he had sauntered out and driven away.

'I heard him say he's headed for Carlisle!' Tessa snorted with an angry pout and a triumphant punch through the air between them.

'I bet you have done this before,' said Clare.

'Not with a stiff,' said Tessa. 'Although I did once leave a punter gasping for breath outside the hospital and did a bunk, and I have no idea what became of him.'

'It's like you don't think of them as human…'

'Oh, blah, blah,' said Tessa. 'Are we here again, Clare? What do *you* think of them as, then? God-like? *Untouchable?* She leaned into her friend with a jab of her plastic sugar stirrer. 'One of them is dead, and I have Shannon to think about.'

There had been abortions and miscarriages and then there was Shannon. Clare couldn't think of Tessa's teenage daughter in any other way. She couldn't remember why, of all the foetuses, she was the one destined to be born; and she would have pitied her, had the fruits of Tessa's labours not furnished her with the sort of lavish lifestyle that turned teenage girls into really rather odious little bitches. Shannon was as liable to sneer at Clare as her mother, only with the wrinkle of a pierced nose instead of a powdered one. And Shannon was already on sexual conquest number four.

'Think of Tilly, only more loveable and worthwhile,' said Tessa, as Clare had been silently attempting to conjure a positive picture of Tessa's daughter. 'That's what having a kid is all about. And I have to protect her from all this crap.' Tessa shored herself up inside what Clare thought of as her trademark suede jacket. ' *We* have to protect her now.'

They drove on to the quarry where they giggled at how easy it was to lift a body out of their car—rolled up and gaffer-taped inside a rug—and chuck it over the edge. Clare thought of a comedy sketch on her parents' black-and-white TV featuring two men and a plank. There wasn't another car or an onlooker for miles.

'I feel like bloody Lady Macbeth,' said Tessa on the precarious lip of the quarry, holding her arms wide to reveal the full potential of their fringed wings. 'Only with the balls to get the job done!'

Her pretend wings were poor substitutes for the real thing, it seemed, as Clare launched her hands into the small of her back and sent her flying over the edge to join the married, naked, dead man wrapped in Clare's bedroom carpet. Tessa's lungs released the most convincing orgasmic moan her best friend had ever heard from her as she spun head over limbs into the dusty abyss below.

Clare clambered breathlessly back into Tessa's jeep where the tree-shaped air freshener twirled manically in her face.

She had been deluded, all these years. She muttered to herself that Tilly *was* worthwhile—at least as some slutty teenager—and Dan *wasn't* desperate.

She leaned back onto the sheepskin headrest for a moment to still the pounding in her chest, and to luxuriate in the rising flames of pleasure in her groin as she reconciled what she had done with what she might do next.

The End

Other titles from Sasha Faulks

Loving Amélie

Born Slowly

The Garrow Boy

Trees and Men

Soul Girl

Available from Amazon on Kindle and in paperback

,

25501709R00045

Printed in Great Britain
by Amazon